SPEED DEMON

FRED BOWEN

PEACHTREE
ATLANTA

Published by
PEACHTREE PUBLISHING COMPANY INC.
1700 Chattahoochee Avenue
Atlanta, Georgia 30318-2112
www.peachtree-online.com

Edited by Vicky Holifield
Cover design by Nicola Simmonds Carmack
Composition by Melanie McMahon Ives

Printed in May 2019 in the United States of America by LSC Communications in Harrisonburg, Virginia

10 9 8 7 6 5 4 3 2 1 (hardcover)
10 9 8 7 6 5 4 3 2 1 (trade paperback)
First Edition

HC 978-1-68263-076-1
PB 978-1-68263-077-8

Library of Congress Cataloging-in-Publication Data

Names: Bowen, Fred, author.
Title: Speed demon / written by Fred Bowen.
Description: First edition. | Atlanta : Peachtree Publishing Company Inc., [2019] | Summary: "Ninth-grader Tim Beeman, struggling as a newcomer at elite Hilton Prep, is torn between using his special talent for speed by playing on the prestigious football team or by running with the more relaxed track and field team" —Provided by publisher.
Identifiers: LCCN 2018052938| ISBN 9781682630761 (hardcover) | ISBN 9781682630778 (trade pbk.)
Subjects: | CYAC: Running—Fiction. | Speed—Fiction. | Ability—Fiction. | Preparatory schools—Fiction. | Schools—Fiction.
Classification: LCC PZ7.B6724 Spe 2019 | DDC [Fic]—dc23 LC record available at *https://lccn.loc.gov/2018052938*

For my Friday reading group at
Woodlin Elementary—

Aaron Boissiere
Adam Levy
Andrew St. Clair
Jacob Wexler

CHAPTER 1

Tim Beeman stared down the Hilton Prep track. *Fifty yards,* he thought. *Fifty yards and a chance to show everyone what "the new kid" can do.*

At the starting line, Mr. Salerno, the physical education teacher, instructed the runners: "Beeman and Bland, you're next up. Butler and Cavanaugh, get ready!"

Tim shook out his arms and legs. Even though it was still summer, the morning air held a taste of fall. He ran in place for a few seconds, lifting his legs almost to his chest.

Tim slipped his feet into the starting blocks and placed his fingers along the starting line like an Olympic sprinter. *Nice and smooth,* he reminded himself. *No need to rush things. You've got plenty of speed. You can show all these Hilton kids what you can do.*

Tim looked down at the composite surface under his feet. *It'll be fun to run on a nice track like this.* His arms and legs tensed as he waited for the call. Two more teachers, Mr. Rivera and Mr. Carpenter, stood fifty yards down the track, holding stopwatches.

"On your mark...get set...go!"

Tim burst out of the blocks, leaving Bland in his dust. At ten yards he was moving at full speed—legs churning, arms pumping, feet barely touching the track. Tim felt the wind in his face as he ran toward the bright light of the early morning sun.

As Tim flashed by Mr. Carpenter, he heard the click of the stopwatch. Tim slowed to a stop some twenty yards past the finish line, took a deep breath, rested his hands on his hips, and turned around.

Mr. Carpenter stood next to Mr. Rivera. They were both staring at the watch. Then the two men looked at each other.

"Would you mind running that again?" Mr. Carpenter asked Tim.

"Sure, no problem."

"Whenever you feel ready."

Tim walked slowly back to the starting line. *I must have run a pretty good time if they want me to run it again,* he thought. He stole a glance at the other runners waiting to race. They looked pretty impressed with "the new kid."

"Let Beeman run it again!" Carpenter shouted to Salerno. "After he catches his breath." Mr. Salerno waved in agreement.

Tim could hear the line of runners buzzing with talk about his run.

"Man, Bland looked like he was running in cement."

"Beeman must have beat him by twenty yards...easy."

"He was really flying!"

"Did they tell you your time?" asked a kid near the end of the line.

Tim shook his head. "They just told me to run it again."

A short, chunky kid grabbed Tim by the shoulders and shoved him into the front spot in line. "Take my place," he said. "I'm not running against you. No way. You got some serious speed. You'll make me look like a complete loser. Even worse than Bland."

"All right, Fullmer and Beeman," called Mr. Carpenter. "Next up."

The second race was just like the first. Tim was at top speed within a few strides and flashed across the finish line in a blur. *That one may be even faster,* he thought as he heard Mr. Carpenter click the stopwatch.

This time after Tim slowed down, he took a moment and looked around the Hilton Prep track and football field. The concrete stands looked like a miniature professional stadium, a lot nicer than the field at Tim's old school. A big scoreboard proclaiming that it was "A Gift from the Viking Class of 2009" stood blank at the back of the end zone.

Tim turned around. Again the two coaches were huddled over the stopwatch.

"Hey, Beeman!" Mr. Carpenter called out. "Do you always run like this?"

Tim shrugged. "I guess. I've always been pretty fast."

"Pretty fast?" Carpenter repeated. "Kid, you just set the school record for the 50-yard dash for a freshman."

"Really?" Tim knew he was fast but...a school record?

"Yeah, really. That record has been around for something like ten years."

Tim smiled to himself. *Maybe a record in the 50-yard dash will make some of these stuck-up Hilton kids notice me. I might even get on one of the teams.*

So far, being a ninth-grade "new kid" was no fun. Tim hardly had anyone to talk with and nobody at Hilton knew who he was. But maybe that was about to change.

After a quick shower, Tim got back into his Hilton Prep uniform—khakis and a dark blue golf shirt with the Hilton Prep insignia on the front pocket.

As he walked out of the locker room, he

glanced up at a big board that listed the Hilton Prep running records by class. A piece of masking tape had already been placed over the square for the freshman 50-yard dash. It read: Timothy Beeman 6.10.

Freshman Boys

50 Yards	Timothy Beeman	6.10
100 Yards	Justin Caldwell	10.52
200 Yards	Walter Chwals	22.29

The other kids coming out of the locker room noticed it too.

A tall boy stopped right next to Tim. "Hey, look," he said. "A couple of days in school and this guy's already on the big board."

"Right," the boy standing behind him said. "Beeman's the man...the new champ."

"What else can you do?" asked the tall boy. "Leap tall buildings in a single bound?"

Tim smiled. Looked like things were changing already. He wished he could tell his mother.

CHAPTER 2

Tim looked across the Hilton Prep lunchroom and felt a familiar nervous feeling in the pit of his stomach. The first couple of days he'd sat alone, eaten quickly, and headed straight to the library. *This is the worst part of being the new kid,* he thought. *Figuring out where to sit at lunch.*

"Hey, Tim!"

He barely heard the voice over the noise of trays clattering and kids talking.

"Hey, Tim. Over here!"

Tim spotted Marquis Newhouse, the kid who sat behind him in Ms. Lin's math class, standing and waving him over to the other side of the room. Tim weaved his way through the crowd of ninth and tenth graders, dodging their lunch trays. He finally reached the edge of the big room.

"I figured you could use a place to sit," Marquis said as he pulled out a chair. "The lunchroom is the worst." He gestured toward a girl sitting at the table. "You know Sophia Singh? She's the math whiz of the ninth grade."

Sophia made a face like she was tired of people talking about how smart she was.

Tim set his lunch tray on the table and sat down.

"Have you figured out this place yet?" Sophia asked, changing the subject.

"Not really," Tim admitted. "It's tough learning everybody's names. And it doesn't help that just about everyone is wearing the exact same outfit."

Marquis took over, pointing around the room with his fork. "All right, we'll give you a quick rundown. The athletes sit in the middle of the lunchroom by teams—"

"You *have* figured out that Hilton Prep is

a huge sports school, right?" Sophia interrupted. "Jocks rule."

"No question about it," Marquis continued. "Football is king, so those guys sit right in the middle. Basketball is close by. Then baseball."

"The lacrosse guys are over there," Sophia said. "They think they're hot stuff, but—"

"But they're just guys who aren't big enough or fast enough to play football," Marquis said, finishing her thought. "They sit a couple of tables away."

"What about the girls?" Tim asked. "Do they sit by teams too?"

"Not as much," Sophia explained. "Some sit with the guys they like, but mostly they sit with their friends. It can get pretty cliquish."

Tim unwrapped his sandwich and took a bite. He wasn't sure he'd ever figure out his new school.

"What about you guys?" he asked. "Do you play anything?"

"Track and field," Marquis said. "It's not a big deal."

"That's why we're sitting back here in the corner," Sophia explained with a laugh.

"But you should come out for track," Marquis continued. "It's a lot of fun. And we need more kids."

"When are tryouts?"

"No tryouts," Sophia said. "Everybody makes it. Like he said, we need the kids."

"All sports start next week," Marquis explained.

"None of the official teams practice the first week," Sophia said, shaking her head. "It's like they're trying to pretend Hilton isn't a jock school."

Marquis laughed. "Yeah, right."

Tim went back to eating his sandwich.

"Whoa, heads up," Marquis said, sounding a little startled. "Hawk at eleven o'clock. Something big must be happening for *him* to come down off his mountain and into the lunchroom."

"Who's Hawk?" Tim asked.

"Coach Hawkins," Sophia said in a low voice. "He's been the head varsity football coach here for twenty-something years. He practically runs the place."

"Look, he's coming over here," Marquis said.

"You're kidding." Sophia turned around in her chair to get a better look, then swung back to face them. "You're right, he is coming this way. What could he want with us?"

In a moment, Coach Hawkins stood above their table, dressed in pressed khakis and a blue Hilton golf shirt with "Coach Hawkins" stitched into the breast pocket. His shoulders were squared back and he looked Tim right in the eye.

"Are you Timothy Beeman?"

"Yes sir," Tim answered. Coach Hawkins seemed like one of those guys you just had to call "sir."

"I'm Coach Hawkins," he said, shaking Tim's hand. "I'm the head varsity football coach around here. I've heard about you."

Marquis and Sophia looked at each other and then at Tim. Their jaws were almost hitting the lunch table in surprise.

Tim didn't know what to say so he let Coach Hawkins do the talking.

"I heard you broke the school record for the 50-yard dash this morning during your PE class."

"What?" Sophia blurted out. "You didn't tell us that!"

"Well, he did," Coach continued with a small smile. "Ran it in 6.10 seconds. It's up on the big board if you don't believe me."

"You can't be serious," Marquis said. "In 6.10?"

Ignoring him, Coach got right down to business. "Ever play football, Timothy?"

Tim shook his head. "Not really. I mean not on a real team. I've...you know...played touch football at the park. But my mom didn't want me to play tackle."

Coach's smile got bigger. "Maybe I can talk to your mother."

"Um...she died three years ago...when I was eleven." Tim felt funny talking about his mother in front of kids he had just met. Truth was, he didn't talk to anyone about his mom, except sometimes his dad.

The news seemed to knock the coach off balance. "I'm...I'm sorry...really sorry to hear that. Maybe I could talk with your dad or—?"

"Oh yeah," Tim said quickly. "My dad likes football. We watch the games on TV and throw the ball around sometimes."

"How are you at catching the ball?"

"Pretty good," Tim said, trying not to brag. "I mean, if I can get my hands on it, I can usually hold on to it."

Coach Hawkins rested his hand on Tim's shoulder. "That sounds good to me. Tryouts start on Monday. Coach Flores is in charge of the junior varsity. He can teach you how it's done. We would love to see you out there. The Vikings can always use someone with your speed."

"Hey, man. Maybe you don't want to be out there with all those big guys hitting you," Marquis said in a low voice. "Stick with track."

"Son, Tim here is so fast, no one's going to catch him." Coach Hawkins laughed as he walked away.

Tim took another bite of his sandwich and gulped down the last of his milk.

Marquis leaned back in his chair. "Let me get this straight," he said. "You set the school record for the 50-yard dash. You have a personal interview with the Hawk in which he practically begs you to play football. And it's your first week at Hilton Prep?"

Marquis looked at Sophia. "Can you believe it? We've got us a celebrity here—an honest-to-goodness Hilton Prep celebrity—at our lunch table!"

"Come on, it's not that big a deal," Tim protested.

"It's not that big a deal? The legendary Hawk came looking for you. He knows your name. Hawk doesn't know me and I've been at Hilton since second grade."

"So are you going out for football?" Sophia asked Tim.

"I don't know."

Marquis frowned. "Are you kidding me?" he said. "Of course he'll go out for football. At Hilton Prep, football is king!"

CHAPTER 3

"Hey Tim, could you bring me the cayenne pepper?" Tim's father called from across the kitchen.

"The what?"

"The cayenne pepper. Look in the spice drawer."

Mr. Beeman stood at the counter staring at a cookbook as Tim rummaged through a drawer filled with spice containers.

"Is it this red stuff?" Tim asked, holding up a small jar.

"Yeah, that's it. Great. Now set the oven at 375 degrees."

"What are you making?"

"Pecan-encrusted tilapia," Tim's dad answered proudly. "The recipe sounds really good."

Tim wasn't so sure. He preferred hamburgers or pizza to fish.

But the dish turned out to taste a lot better than it sounded.

"Hey, this isn't bad," Tim said after his first bite of the flaky fish.

"You sound surprised," Tim's father said. "You didn't believe your dad could do anything but make spaghetti or grill hamburgers. O ye of little faith."

The candles on the table flickered as the two continued eating and talking. Tim's mother had loved candles at dinner, and he and his father still always ate dinner by candlelight.

"How's school going?"

"I guess I'm getting used to it."

"Well, it's only the first week. It might take a while."

"It's kind of tough meeting kids," Tim admitted. "Coming to the school in the ninth grade. I mean...everybody's already in a group."

"How's lunch period going?" Dad asked. "I remember that was the hardest when I

16

moved. The big question was always 'Who do I sit with?'"

"I sat by myself the first couple of days but today I sat with Marquis and Sophia, kids from my math class." Tim took another bite of the tilapia and continued. "Hilton Prep is way different from Central. Sports are huge at Hilton. Most of the kids hang out with their teammates."

"Maybe you should try out for something," Mr. Beeman suggested. "Like track. You've always been a fast runner."

"Oh, that reminds me. They timed us in gym class today, and I set the school record for freshmen for the 50-yard dash."

Tim's father almost dropped his fork. "You're kidding me! What was your time?"

"I ran it in 6.10 seconds."

"Whoa!" Mr. Beeman sounded impressed. "That should get you on the track team."

"Actually, the varsity coach wants me to try out for the junior varsity football team."

"You mean that guy Hawkins? I've heard he's the head honcho in Hilton sports. What did you tell him?"

"I told him about Mom."

"Did you tell him she was a doctor and treated a lot of kids who got hurt playing football?"

Tim shook his head. "I didn't go into all that. I just told him she didn't want me to play football."

Tim and his father sat in silence for a while. It had been three years since Tim's mother died of cancer. They'd stayed in their old house for a while, but this past summer when his father was promoted, they'd moved to another city. So now Tim was in a new school, a fancy private school. "A fresh start," his father had called it. Lots of things were different at his new school and in their new house, but the reality of his mom being gone was always close by.

Tim's father finally took a deep breath. "One thing I've learned in the last three years," he said in a soft tone, "is that it's you and me now. *We* have to make our own decisions."

He pushed his chair away from the table and popped his last bite of fish into his mouth. "So what do *you* think?" he asked.

Tim thought for a moment. "I'd kind of like to try football," he said. "But I'm not sure. I mean, I've never really played the game."

"With your speed, the coaches will most likely put you at wide receiver," his father said. "You could make a pretty good one."

Tim laughed. "Coach Hawkins said I was so fast they'd probably never touch me."

"That reminds me of your grandfather. He was a big fan of 'Bullet Bob' Hayes of the Dallas Cowboys." Mr. Beeman smiled as he recalled the details. "Hayes was an Olympic gold medalist sprinter in the 1964 Games. Then he got drafted by the Cowboys in one of the later rounds. He was the fastest guy in football. Your grandfather said he was so fast nobody could cover him one-on-one. The teams started playing more zone defenses because of him."

Tim's father poured himself a little white wine. He wasn't finished talking about old-time football players. "Then there were Darrell Green and Deion Sanders. They were defensive backs and super fast. Green was the fastest guy in the NFL for years. These days they've got lots of fast guys. I wonder who's considered the fastest now."

He smiled at the memories. "Your granddad and I used to watch football together all the time. Of course, all those guys like Hayes, Green, and Sanders were *real* football players. They weren't just sprinters."

Tim knew his father enjoyed remembering all the old players. The two of them still tried to watch some NFL games together every weekend during the season. Tim was sure his dad would be happy if he decided to go out for the junior varsity team. Still, he also knew his dad would never pressure him about it.

"When are tryouts?" his dad asked.

"They start Monday," Tim said.

His dad glanced over at him. "You could try it and see if you like it. Sounds like Coach Hawkins thinks you'd be pretty good."

"I don't know. Maybe I will. The JV coach, Mr. Flores, is supposed to be a good guy." Tim sat and stared at the flickering candles, thinking. "And it might be a good way to meet more kids at school," Tim said finally. "You know, break into a group."

His dad smiled. "That's a pretty solid reason to play. I think your mother would understand that."

Tim nodded. He was warming up to the idea of playing football at Hilton Prep. After all, football was king. Being one of the kings was going to be way better than being the new kid.

Mr. Beeman looked out the windows. The late summer sky was turning orange with the sinking sun. He hooked his thumb toward the back door.

"Come on. We can leave the dishes until later. Get the football and let's throw it around while we still have some light left."

Tim popped up from the table and grabbed the football from the corner of the kitchen. He followed his dad outside into the fading evening.

CHAPTER 4

On the first Monday of football tryouts, the Hilton JV coaches wrote down a lot of numbers: Height. Weight. Sizes for every imaginable piece of football equipment. Speed in the 40-yard dash.

Tim was five feet eight inches tall and weighed 151 pounds. He wasn't the smallest kid trying out and certainly wasn't the biggest.

But he was definitely the fastest. Tim could almost feel Coach Flores smiling at him when he flashed across the finish line in the forty. He saw the coach showing the stopwatch to Mr. Morris, the assistant coach in charge of the wide receivers, like a proud father.

Later, Coach Morris took all the players who were trying out for wide receivers and defensive backs to a far corner of the practice field. He had them stand at attention wearing just their Hilton football helmets, shorts, and a dark blue Hilton T-shirt. No pads and no real hitting…yet.

"All right, listen up. Here's the passing tree." Coach Morris handed each player a single sheet of paper. "It has the seven patterns we'll run this year. We're going to practice them until you know them in your sleep. Starting right now."

Tim stared at the diagrams and words on the sheet.

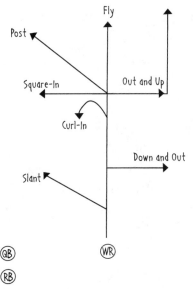

This is going to be a lot trickier than watching the games on TV, he thought, staring at the sheet. The other kids seemed to know what they were doing. Tim decided he'd just watch them and do what they did.

Coach Morris was still talking. "The key to running these patterns is to run them quickly, but with sharp, precise turns so that you get separation from the defensive back."

He turned to the other group of players—the defensive backs. "You guys have to do your best to stay with the receiver. You've got to close in fast when he makes his cut."

Then he held the football above his head. "But remember," he said, addressing both groups, "sometimes it all comes down to who wants the ball the most. You *have* to want the ball more than the other guy. All right, let's go to work!" He sounded his whistle and tossed the ball to one of the team quarterbacks.

Tim and the other receivers ran the patterns over and over in the hot, late August sun with the dust rising from the field. Coach Morris and Hilton's quarterbacks—including the top JV quarterback, Cody Lewis—took turns calling the plays and throwing the passes.

Tim found out right away that speed was not the only skill a wide receiver needed. On his first pattern, a simple down and out, he stumbled as he made his turn toward the sideline and the ball went whizzing past him.

Coach Morris pulled him aside. "You don't have to go top speed all the time," he explained. "Cruise along at about three-quarter speed on your way out, plant your left foot, and then cut hard and turn on the jets. That will give you plenty of separation." He knocked lightly on the top of Tim's helmet.

On another pass—a quick slant—Tim dropped a ball that was right in his hands because he was looking out for the defensive backs.

"Look the ball into your hands!" Coach

Morris shouted. "Don't have your head on a swivel, looking around for the defensive backs. Focus on the ball."

Slowly Tim started to catch on, timing his cuts, using his speed, and looking the ball into his hands. Coach Morris seemed pleased.

Near the end of practice, Tim dropped back into a mini huddle with Cody and another kid trying out for wide receiver.

"Left end slant, right end deep post on two," Cody said in a clear, confident voice.

Tim jogged out to his position on the right side of the field, going over the deep post pattern in his head. He eyed the defensive back about ten yards in front of him. *He's giving me plenty of room,* he thought, *because of my speed.*

"Ready...set...hut one...hut two!"

Tim burst off the line of scrimmage and ran straight at the defensive back, who was backing up quickly.

Coach Morris counted off. "One Mississippi...two Mississippi..." There was no pass rush, but according to the rules of the drill, the quarterback had to throw by the count of three Mississippi.

Tim leaned to the right as he got closer to the defensive back, trying to make him think he would cut in that direction. Just after two Mississippi, Tim planted his right foot into the turf and angled hard toward the goalposts in the distance.

Now Tim was running at top speed, racing by the defensive back as if he was nailed to the ground.

Tim looked back. The ball was already in the air, sailing far down the field. For a moment he thought it might be too far to reach, but he somehow sprinted even faster. The ball settled softly into his hands.

Tim ran another ten yards down the field with the ball tucked under his arm, thinking *Touchdown!* He turned and saw Coach Morris clapping his hands.

"Great throw, Cody!" the coach shouted. "That's how to air it out. Great cut, Tim! Way to use your speed."

Then he turned to the defensive back, who was moving toward the sidelines shaking his head.

"That's okay, Jason, you did all right." Then he added with a huge smile, "Beeman's just a hard man to cover one-on-one."

CHAPTER 5

A couple of weeks later Tim looked around the Hilton Prep cafeteria, eyeing the tables at the edge of the big room. *I wonder where Marquis and Sophia are,* he thought.

"Hey, Beeman!" called a boy from one of the middle tables. "Stop looking around like a doofus and come over here."

Tim glanced over. He didn't recognize the face as much as he recognized the voice. It was a quarterback's voice—strong and confident like he was barking out signals.

Tim walked slowly, almost carefully, toward the football team's table. He wasn't 100 percent certain what to expect.

"Come on, sit down," Cody said as he

kicked out a chair to open up a spot at the table. "If I'm going to throw touchdown passes to you all season, the least you can do is eat lunch at the team table."

Cody turned to the others. "You know Terrance Jackson, our best running back. T.J.'s going to gain a million yards this season. And Calvin Miller over there is our middle linebacker." He leaned over and cupped his hand over his mouth as if he were whispering a secret to Tim. "Don't get Cal mad at you. He'll break you in two. The dude is major league strong."

T.J. and Calvin chuckled and traded fist bumps with Tim. "Hey, Tim. Good to see you."

Cody pointed at a couple of girls sitting on the other side of the table. "And these two lovely ladies are Ashley Pierce and Alexis Tierney. They're two of the best lacrosse players in the school. But their main job is to keep me in line."

Ashley rocked back and gave Cody a sideways look. "Oh, really? Then we aren't doing a very good job," she said. Alexis just rolled her eyes.

"Oh, I'd be much worse," Cody said, "if you ladies weren't around."

"Worse?" Ashley almost fell off her chair laughing. "That's hard to imagine."

Cody didn't let Ashley's teasing slow him down. "Tim here is my new wide receiver." He grabbed Tim by the back of the neck. "He's got some serious wheels. I mean, this man is fast."

"Two weeks of practice and I cannot over-throw this guy." Cody stood up and thrust his arm out as if he was throwing a long bomb. "Swear to God, no exaggeration. I throw the ball fifty yards downfield, and Tim here is so fast he has to come back ten yards to get it."

Tim saw T.J. and Cal trading glances. It was clear they had heard all this from Cody before.

"I'm telling you, my man Tim is a speed demon," Cody declared.

"You mean Speed *Beeman,*" T.J. said.

Cody pointed at T.J. and smiled. "I like it...Speed Beeman. Believe me, we are going to use this man's speed this season. Big-time."

"Who do you guys play first?" Ashley asked.

Cody took out his phone.

"Hey! You know you're not supposed to use your phone at lunch," Ashley warned. "It's against the rules."

"Yeah, they want us to have conversations, like ladies and gentlemen," Alexis added.

Cody tried to look casual, as if he wasn't worried, but Tim noticed that he slipped the phone below the table where it would be hard to see. "What are they going to do?" he asked. "Arrest me?"

"They could take away your phone," Calvin said.

"No way," he said, looking around the room. "Anyway, Mr. Kelly has lunch duty today. That old dude is as blind as a bat."

Cody pulled up the Hilton Prep JV football schedule. Everyone at the table crowded in to look at the list of schools.

Hilton Prep Vikings
Junior Varsity Football Schedule
All games will be played on Thursdays at 3 p.m.

September 26	Somerset School	Home
October 3	Sunrise Academy	Away
October 10	Saint Raphael's	Home
October 17	King Academy	Away
October 24	Hoover High School	Away
October 31	Franklin Prep	Home
November 7	Marshall High School	Away
November 14	Saint Andrew's	Home

"Okay, so we open with Somerset," Cody pointed out.

"They're pretty good," T.J. said.

"Not that good," Cody said with a wave of his hand. "We'll beat 'em. No problem."

The boys studied the rest of the schedule. "You've got to admit that King Academy is good," Calvin said.

Ashley smothered a laugh with her hand. "Like Cody would ever admit anyone was better than Hilton."

"They're okay," Cody said.

"*Okay?*" T.J. protested. "Their varsity crushed us 34–6 last year!"

Cody wasn't buying it. "Yeah, but that's varsity, not JV."

"And where do you think they get their varsity guys?" Ashley asked.

Before Cody could answer, Cal jumped in. "I think they get those King guys from some kind of crazy Frankenstein laboratory. I mean, those guys are monsters!"

"No worries," Cody said, as calm as could be. "We've got speed this year. Speed Beeman. I'm telling you, those big guys will never catch him."

"Yeah, but if they do," Cal said, "they'll break him in half."

Tim cringed at Cal's warning. He stared at the list of schools. Most of the names didn't mean anything to him. "What about Franklin or Marshall or those Saint schools? Are they any good?"

"They all stink!" Cody declared, throwing up his hands. Everyone at the table burst out laughing, shaking their heads. T.J. tossed a wadded-up napkin at Cody, who caught it and flicked it right back.

Tim kept thinking about the other schools on the schedule. He'd seen Franklin Prep once when his dad was showing him around their new town. It was a huge school with an unbelievable stadium. Tim wasn't so sure Franklin would be an easy opponent. In fact, despite what Cody said, he had a feeling that this wouldn't be an easy football season.

The first game was still a couple of weeks away. He'd worry about wins and losses later. For now, Tim was just glad to be sitting at the table with the team.

CHAPTER 6

Mike Moretti, the Vikings' other wide receiver, pounded his fists on Tim's shoulder pads.

"Hey, take it easy," Tim said. "You don't want to hurt me before the first game."

"The guys at Somerset aren't going to take it easy on you," Mike said. "I promise you that."

Tim jogged in place on the sidelines, breathing deeply. The four weeks of Hilton practices hadn't included a lot of hard hitting. Coach Flores didn't want anybody getting hurt. Defensive backs wrapped their arms around the receivers but didn't smash them to the ground. It was more like a fun game of touch football in the park.

But today was going to be different. Today was the real thing. Maybe that was why he could feel his heart pumping wildly underneath all his football equipment. Tim shook his hands at his sides, trying to settle his nerves.

"Real hitting today," Calvin said as he paced up and down the sidelines. "No more dancing around." He spit on the ground. "Real hitting."

Squinting against the late September sun, Tim took in the scene at the Hilton Prep football stadium. Pockets of fans dotted the stands. He figured it was a pretty good crowd for a JV game.

Marquis and Sophia were sitting in the first row. Tim gave them a quick wave.

Sophia noticed and pointed him out to Marquis. They both stood and shouted, "Let's go, Beeman! Let's go, Vikings!"

Coach Flores brought the team in. "Okay, guys. This is what we've been waiting for. What we've been working for. First game. Let's be aggressive." Flores made a fist and continued. "Go right after them. Don't back down. Play every play right through the whistle. Forty minutes of hard-hitting Hilton football!"

The circle of blue helmets was bouncing up and down. Tim could feel the excitement in the huddle.

"Let's go, Hilton!"

"Forty minutes!"

"Come on, Vikings! No letup."

Coach Morris pulled Tim and Mike over. "Remember, sharp cuts. Get separation from the defensive back," he said, almost breathless. "Give Cody a good target. You've got to want to get the ball more than the other guy."

The teams started off slowly. The offensive players seemed unsure, almost nervous. In the first quarter there were more punts than first downs.

Early in the second quarter, Cody called Tim's number. "Wide right," he said. "Curl in on two."

Just as it was drawn up on the passing tree, and just as he had practiced so many times in the past few weeks, Tim ran eight yards straight upfield toward the retreating defensive back, planted his right foot, and curled in toward the middle of the field.

The ball plunked against his pads. Tim held on and ducked to the ground as a Somerset linebacker whizzed over him.

The referee signaled first down.

"Good catch," Cody said back in the huddle. "Good thing you got down. That linebacker would've torn your head off."

Hilton made another first down on a couple of T.J. runs. Tim noticed that the Somerset defensive back was playing a little closer.

Cody had noticed too. "That defensive back is playing you tight, Speed," he said. "Let's make him pay."

Cody looked around, then called the play. "Fake 34, wide right fly on two."

Tim eyed the defensive back as he jogged to his wide receiver position near the right sideline. The back moved a step closer.

"Hut one...hut two..."

Tim started off at three-quarter speed to trick the defensive back into thinking he wasn't part of the play. Five yards out, Tim turned on his sprinter's speed, racing straight upfield. In a few steps, he was past the defensive back and in the clear. Tim looked back and saw Cody letting go of a long pass. The ball hit Tim in stride and popped up into the air for an awful instant. He managed to gather it in and took off. There was no way anyone was going to catch him now.

Touchdown!

Tim's teammates pounded him on the back and the crowd cheered. He felt great.

T.J. plunged over the goal line for the two-point conversion and Hilton led 8–0.

Tim caught another pass later in the half on a down and out and stepped out of bounds after getting a first down.

Neither team scored again before half-time. Hilton still led, 8–0.

I've played a half and I've hardly been hit, Tim thought as he jogged off the field. *Maybe Coach Hawkins was right. Maybe I'm so fast nobody will catch me.*

But Tim soon realized that the second

half was going to be different. The Somerset defensive back was playing him even closer. Every time Tim tried to go out for a pass, the back knocked into him, throwing him off balance. If Tim slipped by the first back, a second defensive back was there to pick him up.

After another punt, Coach Morris came up to Tim on the sidelines. "They're double-teaming you!" Coach Morris shouted. "You've got to fight your way to get open!"

"He's smashing into me every play," Tim explained.

"Find a way."

Tim didn't have much luck getting open. He caught one more pass on another curl in and then was crushed by three Somerset defenders.

Still, Hilton hung on to win, 14–6.

Tim trudged off the field feeling tired and sore from all the second half hits. *Looks like this football thing isn't going to be all fun and games,* he said to himself.

"Good game!" Sophia shouted as the team made their way to the locker room.

Tim could hardly lift his hand to wave.

Coach Morris put his arm around Tim's shoulder. "Good job," he said as he handed him a piece of paper. "Take a look at the stat sheet."

Game 1—Somerset School

Passing:

	C/Atts	Yards	TDs	INTs
Lewis	7/13	121	1	0

Rushing:

	Atts.	Yards	TDs
Jackson	16	77	1
Allen	6	19	0
Lewis	3	10	0

Receiving:

	Recs.	Yards	TDs
Beeman	4	91	1
Moretti	2	22	0
Nowak	1	8	0

Coach beamed. "Four catches, ninety-one yards, and one TD. Not bad for a beginner."

Cody was all smiles too. "One down, seven more to go!" he shouted to the team and then pointed at Tim. "Speed got us on the board. Nobody—and I mean nobody—can cover my man Speed one-on-one. No way, no how."

Tim could see his father in the cluster of parents as the players got closer to the locker room. Cody grabbed Tim by the arm.

"T.J., Cal, and I are going to the varsity game tomorrow night. Want to come?"

"Sure. What time?"

"The game starts at seven. See you there, about quarter of."

Tim was smiling as he walked up to his father. He had almost forgotten his bumps and bruises.

He was happy. Happy about the win. Happy about his four catches and one touchdown. Happy to be invited to the varsity game with the guys.

Maybe this football thing would be okay after all.

CHAPTER 7

A long line of cars was waiting to get into the stadium parking lot, so Tim's father dropped him off a couple of blocks from the Hilton Prep campus. As Tim got out of the car, he saw the stadium lights in the distance.

"About what time will the game be over?" his dad asked.

"I don't know. Probably around nine o'clock."

"Okay, I'll meet you here around then. Text me if you get out before nine. Be good."

"Got it, Dad. Thanks."

The Hilton Prep football stadium was almost filled with students, parents, and just plain football fans. The band was playing some old classic rock song as the cheerleaders roamed the sidelines chanting cheers.

Tim looked around. He could feel the excitement of the crowd in his chest. *This is big-time,* he thought.

He walked along, looking for the other Hilton JV players. Coach Hawkins let the JV players watch the varsity games from the sidelines during home games.

"Hey, Tim!"

Tim looked into the crowd. Sophia and Marquis were sitting with some other kids in the second row near the 50-yard line.

"Come on," Sophia called and waved him over. "Sit up here with us."

"I can't!" Tim shouted back. "The football guys are watching the game from the sidelines." He pointed downfield.

"All right," Sophia said. "You go be a football hero. See you in math class."

When Tim reached the cluster of JV players, Cody's voice rose above the noise of the crowd. "All right! Speed Beeman is in the house. Mr. Touchdown himself. Time to watch some Friday Night Lights."

Tim traded chest bumps and handshakes with the other JV players.

Then Cody pulled him aside and pointed to the field. "Check out Chad Davis, number 84," he said in a dead-serious voice. "He's a senior and Hilton's best wide receiver. He's not as fast as you, but he's good. Play your cards right and get a little bigger and you might take his place next year."

Tim looked out onto the field. The varsity players were a lot bigger than the guys on the JV team. He felt even smaller standing on the sidelines in his regular clothes as the players warmed up in their pads and helmets.

After one or two plays, Tim could see how fast and how strong the players were. Every hit sounded like a clap of thunder. Varsity football was serious stuff.

"They're all pretty fast," Tim said softly to no one in particular.

"Not as fast as you, Speed," Cody said.

"Believe me, nobody out there could catch you."

It was all football talk among the JV players as the Hilton varsity took a 14–10 lead on a thirty-yard run and a touchdown catch by Davis.

"Man, number 54 for Somerset is a beast. He's all over the field."

"Sweet move by Chad Davis. He faked that guy out of his shoes."

"Look at that pass. Cody, you'd better start practicing. These guys can wing it."

"Whoa…nice block. He absolutely pan-caked that guy."

Hilton Prep stretched its lead to 21–10 in the second half and was driving down the field again. Tim could feel the roars of the crowd washing over him. One more touchdown and Hilton would have the game in the bag.

The Hilton quarterback barked out the signals.

"Ready…set…hut…hut…"

Tim's eyes locked on Chad Davis, who was lined up near the right sideline in front of the JV players. He ran ten yards straight upfield, shoulder faked toward the sideline, and cut sharply left to shake himself loose in the middle of the field.

Nice square in, Tim thought.

Just as Davis gathered in the ball, the strong safety from Somerset hit him hard with his right shoulder, smack between the 8 and the 4 on the front of Davis's shirt.

Crack! The sound echoed through the stadium. Davis fell back, still clinging to the ball, and collapsed onto the turf like a rag doll.

"Whoa!" Calvin shouted. "What a hit!"

"That guy really put the hammer on Davis," T.J. added.

"How did he hold on to the ball?" Cody asked with admiration. "I think that's a first down."

Davis lay flat on his back, not moving. The stadium went quiet. Even the cheerleaders stopped cheering. The players stood around silently as Hawk and the team trainer hustled out onto the field and knelt over the fallen player. The trainer seemed to be whispering into Davis's helmet.

"Has he moved yet?" Cody asked.

"I thought I saw his legs move a little," Calvin said.

"I hope he's not hurt bad," T.J. added. "That was a real hit."

Tim said nothing. It was as if the hit by the Somerset safety had stunned him into silence.

Coach Hawkins signaled the Hilton sidelines. Another wide receiver pulled on his helmet and raced into the huddle.

Tim saw Cody watching a man and a woman on the sidelines who were staring out toward the field. The woman's hands were folded in front of her mouth as if in prayer. The corners of her eyes glistened.

"I think that's Chad's mom and dad," Cody said, nodding in their direction.

After several long, silent minutes, Davis pulled his knees up. Two teammates braced their arms underneath his shoulders and lifted him to his feet. Davis wobbled off the field with the trainer and Coach Hawkins beside him. The crowd's applause followed him to the team bench.

Tim studied the Hilton Prep varsity wide receiver. The stunned player sat staring blankly at the trainer, who stood just a foot or two away asking him questions. Davis's parents stayed off to the side, but they were watching intently. The father put his arm around his wife's shoulders and pulled her in close.

"He's okay," Cody said with his usual quarterback's confidence. "He just got a little shook up."

A little shook up? Tim wasn't so sure. Davis looked like he'd been run over by a truck.

The game started up again, but Tim kept his eyes on the injured player. He barely heard the crowd's cheers as Hilton scored another touchdown.

All he could hear in his head were the whack of the strong Somerset safety smashing into Chad Davis's chest and the sickening thud as the Hilton wide receiver hit the ground.

CHAPTER 8

W ant to throw the ball around?" Tim's father asked as he cleared the lunch dishes from the kitchen table.

"Sure, I need to practice my patterns."

"We could go up to Hilton. It's Sunday. There'll probably be nobody there."

Tim's father was right. The Hilton stadium was almost empty. A few walkers and joggers made their way slowly around the track on the cool, gray day.

Tim and his father set up at the 25-yard line near one of the end zones. Tim shuddered as he noticed that they weren't far from where Chad Davis had been hit during Friday night's game. Mr. Beeman went out to the middle of the field, standing in as the quarterback. He held the football in front of him, waiting for Tim to line up on the right at his familiar wide receiver position.

Then he started calling out patterns. Slant...down and out...square in...post... fly...down out and down.

Tim ran all the patterns a bunch of times.

Mr. Beeman mixed in some football advice with his words of praise.

"Nice catch! Way to look the ball into your hands!"

"Make that cut a little sharper."

"Be sure to drag that back foot to let the referee know you got it inbounds."

After one of Tim's particularly successful runs, his dad shouted, "Now I can see why everybody calls you Speed!"

After about thirty minutes of hard practice, Tim started to feel loose. But he saw that his father was rolling his right shoulder. "You okay, Dad?" he asked.

"I'd better call it quits or my arm is going to fall off," Mr. Beeman said, rubbing his shoulder. "Now I know why there aren't any forty-five-year-old quarterbacks in the NFL."

"Tom Brady's almost forty-five," Tim pointed out.

Mr. Beeman let out a real laugh. "I'm definitely not Tom Brady. How are you doing? Ready to go now?"

Tim looked out at the Hilton Prep track. "Not yet," he said. "I think I'll run a few laps."

"Okay then. See you back home."

Tim wandered over to the track. He started off at a jog. Then he began to pick up the pace. He wasn't running at full speed, but he was going fast enough to send him flying by the middle-aged folks on the track.

Tim felt great. No pads, no helmet, and no defensive backs or linebackers trying to take his head off. He felt free.

As he glided around a turn, he saw two familiar figures waving at the end of the track. Tim slowed down to greet them.

"I thought you'd be running patterns instead of running track," Marquis teased.

"I was," Tim said, jogging in place. "But my quarterback got tired and went home."

"Cody was here?" Sophia asked.

"Nah, my dad was throwing passes to me. What are you guys doing here?"

"Getting a run in," Marquis said.

"Coach wants us to run between track practices," Sophia explained. "To stay loose."

"Good advice," Tim said. "Let's go."

The three athletes looped around the track several times. Tim eased off to keep pace with Marquis and Sophia. After a mile or so he was getting bored.

He looked over at his two companions. "Want to race?" he asked.

"Are you kidding me?" Sophia objected, slowing to a stop. "You're the fastest kid in the class...maybe the whole school."

"Come on, you guys are on the track team," Tim said. "You have to be pretty fast. What do you run?"

"Mostly the 400," Marquis said. "And some of the relays."

"The 800," Sophia added. "And sometimes I do relays too."

Tim grinned and eyed his companions. "Why don't we race around the track once? Four hundred meters...and I'll give you a lead."

"How big a lead?" Sophia asked.

Tim walked over and pointed to a starting line that was drawn across the middle of the track. "I'll start here," he said. "You guys go on up ahead."

Marquis and Sophia walked about twenty meters beyond Tim and looked back at him.

"Keep going," Tim said with a flip of his hand.

They walked another ten meters.

"Keep going."

With another five meters, Marquis and Sophia were almost at the first corner. "How about here?" Sophia called back.

"Okay."

Sophia moved up another five meters.

"Whoa!" Tim said. "That's far enough!"

"I'm taking a few more," she said. "Marquis is little faster than I am."

"You guys are killing me," Tim protested.

"We're just trying to make it fair."

"All right, all right," Tim said. "I'll call out the start." Tim watched as Marquis and Sophia took their crouch positions. They were ready to run.

"On your mark!" he yelled. "Get set! Go!"

Tim burst off the starting line, reaching full speed in a few strides. He looked up and saw Marquis and Sophia racing ahead, arms pumping, legs churning. They were moving pretty fast. *This is going to be tougher than I figured,* Tim thought. He began to close the distance as they raced along the backstretch. Twenty meters... fifteen meters...ten meters.

As they came out of the second corner, Marquis and Sophia were running stride for stride about five meters ahead of him with the finish line coming up fast. His legs were burning, but he pulled to the outside and reached down for a final burst of speed. Tim flashed across the finish line a step in front of the other two.

"I cannot believe you beat us!" Sophia gasped as the three racers slowed down and bent over to catch their breath.

Tim straightened up, smiling ear to ear. He felt as good as if he had scored a touchdown.

Maybe better.

CHAPTER 9

Tim slid his tray onto the JV football team's lunch table.

"Good, you're here," Cody said. "We've got a problem with the team."

"What are you talking about?" Tim asked. "We won our first three games." He pulled out his phone and found the team's schedule.

Hilton Prep Vikings
Junior Varsity Football Schedule
All games will be played on Thursdays at 3 p.m.

September 26	Somerset School	Home	W 14–6
October 3	Sunrise Academy	Away	W 26–0
October 10	Saint Raphael's	Home	W 20–0

October 17	King Academy	Away
October 24	Hoover High School	Away
October 31	Franklin Prep	Home
November 7	Marshall High School	Away
November 14	Saint Andrew's	Home

"We've been crushing everybody. The last two games have been shutouts."

"Watch out for Mr. Kelly," Ashley warned. "Remember, he can take your phone away."

"I thought you said he couldn't see past his nose," Tim said.

Ashley smiled. "He's got a pretty long nose."

"My point is," Cody said, getting back to football, "those were easy teams. Look at the schedule. We've got some rough games coming up. Like this Thursday against King Academy. And then Franklin Prep two weeks after that."

"A few weeks ago, you were bragging we were better than all those teams," Tim said.

Cody shrugged. "Yeah, but that was a few weeks ago."

"King is definitely a tough team," Calvin agreed. "But we can take them down."

Cody looked around the table. "We're going to have to score more."

"Yeah, because there's no way we're going to shut out King," T.J. said.

"Wait a minute," Calvin said, his voice rising. "Are you saying we can't stop those King guys?"

Cody held up his hands, trying to make peace with his team's best defensive player. "Just being real, Cal. Just being real."

Then Cody pointed at Tim. "The problem is that teams are figuring out our new secret weapon."

Tim felt self-conscious. His teammates were putting him on the spot. It seemed like everybody at the table was looking at him like he'd done something wrong. "What do you mean?" he asked finally.

"I mean that after you catch a couple of passes," Cody explained, "they double-team you. They put one guy up on the line of scrimmage...right in your face mask. Then they swing another guy over to cover you deep. Am I right?"

Tim had to admit Cody was onto something. And the bruises on Tim's body proved that he was right. In all three games he had caught more passes in the first half. Then the teams had adjusted in the second half by assigning a defensive back to knock Tim around near the line of scrimmage.

"So what can we do?" Tim asked. If there was a way to not get beat up in the second half of each game, he was all for it. Getting hit was no fun.

Cody sat back with a satisfied smile. "Play you at flanker in the backfield and put you in motion."

"And what will that do?" Calvin asked.

Cody shook his head and gave Cal a look. "You guys on defense are so dumb. If Speed isn't at wide receiver, he won't be standing right on the line of scrimmage like a sitting duck for the other team to crush."

He grabbed the salt and pepper shakers and explained his plan while moving the shakers around like players on a football field. "Speed will be a couple of yards off the line of scrimmage…and moving. So he'll have a few steps to use his speed and his moves to slip by the first defender without getting crunched every time."

Tim smiled. "Sounds good to me. I don't exactly love getting hit."

Cody reached into his backpack and pulled out a notebook. "I've got a couple of plays right here," he said. He placed two neatly drawn diagrams on the table.

"Finish those Tater Tots!" he said, barking orders to T.J., who was reaching toward the papers. "I don't want you getting grease all over my beautiful plays."

T.J. popped his last three Tater Tots in his mouth and grabbed a napkin as the group pressed in around the diagrams.

Flanker Motion Right Square In

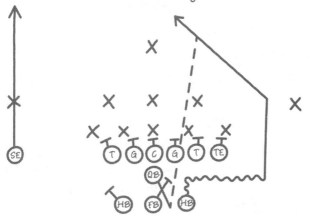

Flanker Motion Right Post

"The first one is flanker motion right, square in," he said, pointing at the diagram. "Tim will start in the backfield, go in motion to the right, and then run a square in. But he can run any of his patterns off this play."

Cody then pointed at the second diagram. "See, this one is flanker motion right, post. No one's fast enough to stay with Speed when he's already moving."

When he was finished, Cody looked around the table. "So what do you think?"

"I like it," T.J. said. "Tim's moving, not starting from a dead stop. That'll make him even harder to cover."

"Right!" Cody exclaimed. "I'm telling you, guys on offense are smart."

Calvin wasn't buying that. "If you guys on offense are so smart," he said, "why do you need new plays while the guys on defense are pitching shutouts?"

Cody didn't have an answer for that one.

"Are you going to show your plays to Coach Flores?" Ashley asked Cody.

"Already have."

"What did he say?"

"He loved them! We're going to start practicing them today."

Cody grabbed Tim playfully around the neck and declared, "Ladies and gentlemen, prepare yourselves. We are now going to unleash the Speed Demon!"

CHAPTER 10

Tim took in the view of the Martin Luther King Academy football stadium as the Hilton Prep players stretched. The stands were almost full and it was still fifteen minutes to kickoff.

"Man, the crowd's really psyched for a *JV* game," he whispered to Cody. "I can't even imagine how excited they must get about the varsity games."

"Remember, most of them are here to cheer for the other guys," Cody said. "I told you they'd be a tough team to beat."

Tim quickly found out that Cody was right. The King Crusaders defense didn't wait until the second half to double-team Tim. From the very first play, a defensive back was up on the line of scrimmage.

Back in the huddle, Cody looked around the circle. "Okay, let's try one of the new plays," he said. "Flanker right in motion, square in. On two."

Tim lined up in the backfield. "Ready... set..." As soon as Cody started his signals, Tim jogged out to the right.

On the count of two, the center hiked the ball to Cody, and Tim bolted upfield, slipping by the first King defender. He raced ten yards and then broke sharply toward an open space in the center of the field. Cody's pass hit him right in the hands.

"First down!" the referee called as he signaled with his outstretched arm.

"Let's keep it going," Cody said back in the huddle. "Flanker in motion right, deep curl in. On two."

Again Tim slipped by the first defender and sprinted upfield. The second King defensive back was backpedaling as fast as he could, thinking Tim was going long. Instead Tim dug his right foot into the turf and curled into the center of the field.

Cody's pass was on the money again. Tim turned and dodged a flying tackler. He juked by the King safety and was off to the races. No one was going to catch him.

Touchdown! Hilton led 7–0.

But the Crusaders came back, grinding out yardage on the ground. Even Calvin's fierce tackles couldn't stop them. The long King drive ended with a short plunge that tied the score, 7–7.

The game turned into a shootout with the teams trading scores and neither defense able to stop the other team's offense. In the fourth quarter, Hilton led 21–20, their lead coming on a blocked point-after touchdown by Calvin.

But there was no stopping the Crusaders. In the fourth quarter they drove the length of the field and scored again. The Hilton defense stiffened to stop an attempt at a two-point conversion. King led 26–21.

Coach Flores gathered the Hilton offense at the sidelines. "There are only three and a half minutes left," he said, shaking his right fist. "Keep playing hard! We've got to score on this drive. If we punt we probably won't get the ball back. Let's make something happen out there."

With Cody quickly calling out plays, the Hilton offense started to move down the field.

A pass to Conrad Nowak, the Vikings tight end...

A down and out to Tim...

And a couple of runs by T.J.

First down on the King 34-yard line.

The King crowd was on its feet and chanting, "Dee-fense! Dee-fense! Dee-fense!"

The crowd must have inspired the Crusaders. Cody couldn't connect with Conrad, and two runs by T.J. were stopped for only a yard each. Coach Flores called time-out and Tim glanced at the stadium scoreboard.

"Fourth down, and we have to get at least eight yards for the first down," Coach Flores said to his offense. "Let's go with flanker motion right, square in again. That's been working. Beeman, go down at least ten yards. Remember, you've got to get the first down. Linemen, hold your blocks. Give Cody a clean pocket to throw."

Coach Flores had called Tim's number. Coach Morris grabbed him as the offense went back onto the field. "Remember to go after the ball," he said. "You've got to want it more than the other guy."

The King fans chanted again as the Hilton offense broke its huddle.

"Dee-fense! Dee-fense! Dee-fense!"

Tim lined up in the backfield and went into motion.

"Hut...hut..."

He broke downfield. The King defensive back tried to check him near the line of scrimmage, but Tim slipped by on an inside move. Now he was one-on-one against the second defensive back.

Tim raced downfield ten yards—enough for the first down—and cut sharply toward the middle of the field. He was open and the ball was in the air. *I have to go after it,* he thought.

But at the last instant Tim caught a glimpse of the Crusader safety coming up quick and hard. Instead of reaching for the ball, Tim pulled his arms back and angled his body to avoid being hit.

The football skidded across the turf. Incomplete pass. King ball on downs. Now Hilton's last chance for a big win was gone.

The King defense was celebrating as the Hilton offense walked off the field with their heads down. Cody stood on the sideline with his helmet on his hip and gave Tim a cold stare. Coach Morris glared straight ahead with his arms crossed in front of his chest, not saying a word.

Coach Flores spoke briefly to the team after the game.

"Good game, guys. King is a tough team. Plus we were playing them at home. We played hard. Just came up a little short.

Maybe if we had made another play or two...."

Like the last play, Tim thought as he remembered how he had backed away from the football and the King safety because he didn't want to get hit.

"We played well," Coach Flores said, finishing up. "I'm proud of everybody."

But Tim didn't feel proud. As he walked slowly away, he felt defeated. But even worse, he felt the disappointed looks of Cody and Coach Morris following him every step of the way.

CHAPTER 11

"Ready...set...hut...hut..."

Cody faded back, looking to the left and right for his receivers.

Tim dashed downfield, faked one step to his right, then angled toward the middle of the field on a post pattern. The ball floated into his arms as he raced by the defensive back. He ran a few more yards and slowed down to a trot.

"Hey, Cody. Great pass!" Coach Morris said. "Good fake, good pattern, Tim. You kept your speed up. That's good."

The receivers jogged back and gathered in a small circle around their coach. "Remember to look for the post pattern," Coach Morris instructed. "And notice if the safety's playing up on Tim or if he's a little too slow. Okay, let's run another one."

Tim and the other Hilton wide receivers were running patterns against the team's defensive backs. The offensive and defensive linemen were working out on another part of the practice field.

It was late October. The season was half over, and the days were cooler and getting shorter. The sun was setting behind Bodaken Hall on the Hilton campus, lighting the gray clouds in the evening sky.

Pretty soon we'll be practicing in the dark, Tim thought.

The players kept running patterns—posts, down and outs, square ins, curl ins—as the day faded away. Even when the defensive backs double-teamed Tim, they couldn't stop him from grabbing Cody's passes.

"Remember, no hitting," Coach Morris reminded the players. "I don't want anybody getting hurt in practice."

After a while, he called out, "One more, then let's call it quits for today."

"Flanker in motion right, square in on two," Cody said to the huddled receivers.

Tim lined up behind Cody and went in motion to the right. "Hut...hut..."

Right on cue, Tim slipped by the first defensive back and dashed downfield. At about ten yards, he angled quickly to the middle of the field.

He was open. The ball was almost there. Tim noticed a defensive back coming up fast, but this time he kept going, then reached out and snagged the ball.

"Good grab!" Coach Morris shouted, pumping his fist. "That's how to go and get the ball!" He looked around at the darkened field and the thickening clouds. "Okay, that's it. Let's save some for Thursday against Hoover."

Tim and Cody walked slowly back to the locker room, holding their helmets at their sides by the face masks. The sun was completely blocked by Bodaken Hall and night covered the field.

"Nice throw on that last pattern," Tim said. "It was right on the money."

"Nice catch...this time," Cody responded.

Tim could hear an edge in his teammate's voice. "What do you mean?"

"Same pattern, same throw," Cody said, staring ahead. "But you didn't make the catch against King."

Tim's jaw clenched. He was getting a little tired of Cody always being the quarterback. Always being the lead dog, the big man. On the football field. In the locker room. Even in the lunchroom.

"The pass against King was too far in front of me." Tim knew he wasn't exactly telling the truth, but he wasn't going to let Cody push him around.

Cody stopped walking and turned to look straight at Tim. "The pass was there," he said, almost shouting. "*You* weren't there."

"Hey, why are you two going at each other?" T.J. asked, joining the pair near the locker room door.

"I'm just saying, Tim should have caught that last square in against King."

"Come on. Take it easy," T.J. said. "The game's over. We lost. Save some of this energy for Thursday against Hoover."

But Cody wouldn't let it go. "That was a big play," he said. "Tim should've made it. It was fourth down, our last chance. The game was on the line."

"Maybe I didn't make the catch because I didn't want to get blown up by King's safety!" Tim blurted out. His mind flashed back to Chad Davis lying on the ground weeks before. He remembered how strangely silent the Hilton stadium had become and the looks on the faces of Davis's parents. Sometimes there was a price to pay—a big price—for going for the ball.

"Forget it," T.J. repeated. "It's done now. Concentrate on Thursday."

"I'm just saying," Cody continued in a low, determined voice. "If you want to play football, you have to take the hits. I take them. T.J. takes them. Cal takes them. Real football players take the hits."

Cody's words stopped Tim in his tracks. Like he'd been hit by a linebacker.

Cody and T.J. went on into the school and headed for the locker room. Tim stayed outside for a moment, thinking. Finally he stepped inside and glanced at the big board. There was his name—and his big record.

Freshman Boys
50 Yards   Timothy Beeman   6.10

Real football players take the hits, he thought, repeating Cody's words in his mind.

Maybe you're not a real football player, he told himself. *Maybe you're nothing but a speed demon.*

CHAPTER 12

Tim couldn't concentrate on his math homework. All the sines and cosines were a jumble in his mind. Finally he slammed his book shut.

Cody's words were still bouncing around in his head.

The pass was there. You weren't.

The game was on the line.

Real football players take the hits.

Tim looked at his mother's picture on the dresser. It was a photo from years ago... before she got sick. Tim was just seven years old. They were smiling and holding each other close.

For the millionth time Tim wished she was still here.

Mom would understand, Tim thought. *It's harder to talk to Dad. It's almost like he expects me to like football as much as he does. Of course, he doesn't have to take all the hits.*

Tim walked slowly downstairs and wandered into the kitchen. He absentmindedly opened the refrigerator and kitchen cabinets, looking for something to eat. His father was in the next room, reading and listening to jazz. Tim recognized Miles Davis's muted trumpet. It always sounded so sad.

"How's your homework coming?" Tim's father called.

"Okay. I'm just taking a break."

Tim stepped into the room. His father rested his book on his lap.

"What are you reading?"

His father looked at the cover of the book. "*The Rooster Bar* by John Grisham."

"Any good?"

"It's okay." His father smiled. "Better than watching the shows on TV." He gave Tim a questioning look. "How's football going?"

"Okay, I guess."

"You don't sound so sure."

There was a short pause as Tim thought about Cody and what he had said. Miles Davis's trumpet filled the quiet space.

"Cody got down on me today because I didn't make that last catch against King," Tim said.

"I'm sure he knows you can't catch everything."

"Yeah, but..."

"But what?"

"Maybe..." Tim sat down across from his dad. "Maybe I didn't make the catch because I didn't want to get hit."

"Getting hit is part of the game," his father said. "A *big* part of the game."

"Yeah, that's what Cody said." Tim looked away. "Maybe I just don't like playing the game that much."

Tim was surprised to hear himself say the words—the words he had been thinking all evening—out loud.

Miles Davis played on. His trumpet sounded as if it was coming from some lonely city corner at night, the streetlights reflecting off the wet pavement.

Tim's father took out his phone and clicked on the Hilton JV football team website. He pulled up the team statistics.

Passing:

	Games	C/Atts	Yards	TDs	INTs
Lewis	4	36/68	577	5	2
Hansen	1	0/1	0	0	0

Rushing:

	Games	Atts.	Yards	TDs
Jackson	4	71	361	5
Allen	4	21	92	1
Lewis	4	14	48	1

Receiving:

	Games	Recs.	Yards	TDs
Beeman	4	18	321	3
Moretti	4	8	108	0
Nowak	4	6	76	1
Jackson	4	4	72	1

"Let's see," he started, tilting his glasses a bit. "You've played four games, right?"

"Yeah."

"In four games you got eighteen catches for 321 yards and three touchdowns. Nobody else on the team is even close."

He turned his phone so Tim could see the screen.

"Seems like you're doing pretty well for someone who doesn't like the game."

"I know. Most of the time I do like running and catching the ball, but it just seems like Cody, Calvin, and T.J. all enjoy the game—and the hitting—a whole lot more than I do."

"How many more games do you have?" Tim's father asked.

"Four."

"Tell you what. Why don't you play the rest of the games and see how you feel about football at the end of the season," Tim's father said. Then he added, "I think it's important to finish things you've started...like your homework, for instance."

Tim laughed. "Okay, I get it. Break time's over, right?"

"Right. Break time's over."

Tim stood and slowly made his way up the stairs. Miles Davis's trumpet followed him with every step.

But Tim wasn't thinking about the lonely trumpet sound or his math homework. He was thinking about the next four games and wondering whether, deep in his heart, he really wanted to play them.

CHAPTER 13

Tim blew on his hands to try and get them warm. It was almost the end of October and the season was more than half over. There was a hint of winter in the air. The wind and rain from the previous week had slapped most of the leaves from the trees.

The grass on the Hilton Prep practice field had been worn away by hours of pounding by players' cleats. The ground was hard and unforgiving. Practicing on the field was like playing football on a parking lot. Not much fun.

Cal and T.J. didn't seem to mind any of it. They actually liked playing in the cold.

"Football weather!" Cal shouted as puffs

of his warm breath drifted into the cold air. "*Real* football weather."

"Hitting weather," T.J. agreed, almost laughing. "It's a great day to play."

Great day? Those guys are crazy, Tim said to himself, tensing his shoulders against the frigid air. *At least it's not raining.* He thought back to the team's last game against Hoover High.

The previous Thursday, it had rained from the opening kickoff to the final whistle. A cold, pelting rain. And the wind had whipped wildly around the Hoover stadium.

The wind and rain had made passing the ball nearly impossible. Cody had tried a few short passes early on, but they had fallen incomplete onto the muddy field.

Cody called a wide receiver reverse, trying somehow to get the ball into Tim's hands. But Tim slipped on the slick grass and lost yardage. His speed didn't help much on a sloppy field.

"Forget the fancy stuff," Cody growled in the huddle and then looked at the offensive line. "We're going to have to win this one on the ground."

So they gave up on the passing game and handed the ball to T.J. Play after play they pounded the ball into the middle of the Hoover line. Tim spent almost every play blocking, sloshing around in the mud, or standing on the sidelines wishing his feet were dry.

Hilton Prep won 12–0 on a pair of touchdown runs by T.J. But for Tim the win wasn't much fun.

No catches. No yards. No chance to show off his speed.

"Let's run a couple more plays!" Coach Morris shouted now as he surveyed the practice field. "Then we'd better call it a day."

Tim ran a down and out and then a post pattern. Both times the cold, hard ball smacked against his hands, stinging his frozen fingers. He held on, but just barely.

"Hey, Beeman! In this kind of weather try catching it closer to your body," Coach Morris suggested, "instead of just with your hands."

"Okay, bring it in!" Coach Flores shouted,

waving his clipboard above his head.

The team huddled together at the edge of the practice field. It was so cold that steam rose from some players' heads when they removed their helmets.

Tim stayed back in the last ring of the circle. He bounced up and down on his feet, trying to keep them warm. He cupped his hands around his mouth and blew hot air on them. Nothing seemed to help.

Coach Flores drew the team in closer and started talking. "Franklin Prep always has a solid team. They beat King 20–14, so you know they've got to be good. We're going to have to play hard. Forty solid minutes of football. No letup. It's going to be tough— and they say it's going to be even colder than today."

"Is there any rain in the forecast, Coach?" T.J. shouted with a laugh. "I love playing in the rain!"

Even in the dark Tim could see Coach Flores smiling. "Sorry, T.J., no rain. But that's good. Cody can throw some passes. Maybe get the ball to Tim and Mike too."

The coach held his hands up for quiet. "Get a good night's sleep," he said. "You're going to need all the energy you can muster up tomorrow."

Coach Flores raised a fist and the players pulled in close. They all stretched their right hands toward the coach's fist.

"Hard work on three!" Coach Flores exclaimed. "One! Two! Three!"

"Hard work!" the players shouted in unison. Then they broke out of the circle and headed for the locker room. The *click clack* of their cleats on the pavement filled the night air.

"You're not going to have another week off, Speed," Cody said to Tim as they descended the stairs. "It's going to be hard to run the ball against Franklin."

"You saying we can't run the ball against those guys?" T.J. asked from a couple of steps behind them. Now *he* sounded a little tired of Cody's talk.

"Just being real, T.J.," Cody said. "Franklin's tough. We're going to need Speed this week if we're going to win."

"No worries," Tim said. "I'll be there."

Tim turned and headed into the locker room. *At least I'll be running and catching passes,* he thought, *instead of getting knocked around and blocking the entire game.*

CHAPTER 14

Tim looked around the Hilton Prep stadium. Despite the cold, raw weather, the stands were more than half full. He spotted his father sitting several rows up near the 50-yard line, huddled under a blanket.

He scanned the student section closer to the field. As soon as he located Sophia and Marcus, they spotted him. Sophia stood and shook both her fists. "Come on, Vikings!" she cheered.

Once the game started, it didn't take long for Tim to realize that Coach Flores had been right about the Franklin Tigers. They were good. The Tigers took the opening kickoff and marched downfield, muscling into the end zone on a short run up the middle.

In no time at all the Franklin team was in the lead, 7–0.

The Hilton Prep offense couldn't answer back. For all of T.J.'s brave talk about running the football, he wasn't getting anywhere today. The Franklin defense stuffed the first two runs at the line of scrimmage.

Tim caught a short pass but was tackled before he could take a step. Fourth down and five yards to go. Hilton Prep had to punt.

In fact, Hilton spent most of the first half punting. The Tigers put together another long, time-eating drive near the end of the first half to stretch the lead to 14–0.

At halftime, Coach Flores tried to fire up the discouraged Vikings.

"It's only two touchdowns. We're still in this game!" he shouted. "But we're going to have to open it up a little. Take some chances. Put the ball in the air!"

Hilton Prep got the ball at the beginning of the second half. Cody stepped into the huddle. "Let's try a pass on first down," he said. "Fake 34, flanker right down and out on two."

"Ready…set…hut…hut!"

Cody faked a handoff to T.J. The Franklin defense went for the fake. Then Cody turned and rifled a quick pass to Tim near the right sideline. Tim caught the ball and tiptoed out of bounds for an eight-yard gain.

"Don't step out of bounds!" Cody barked as Tim hustled back to the huddle. "Turn upfield. We need every yard we can get against these guys."

A few plays later, Cody called Tim's number again. Right flanker in motion, curl in.

Tim streaked out twelve yards, stutter-stepped, and darted into an empty space in the middle of the field. The ball thumped against his chest. But before he could take a step, two Franklin defenders sandwiched him in a crushing tackle. Tim dropped to the turf, gasping for breath but still holding the ball.

Tweeeeeet! The referee blew his whistle

and waved his arms above his head. "My time-out."

Coach Morris rushed out and knelt over Tim.

"You okay?" he asked.

Tim could hardly breathe. A sharp pain knifed his right side.

"Can you sit up?"

With help, Tim sat up. In a couple of seconds he started to feel the air coming back into his lungs. Coach Morris motioned to Calvin, who was standing on the sidelines. "Cal, over here! A little help!"

Cal hustled out. He and Coach Morris put their arms underneath Tim's armpits and lifted him to his feet. Tim wobbled to the sidelines, taking a deep breath with each step.

"Tell me when you're ready to go back in," Coach Flores said. "We're going to need you."

Tim looked out onto the field, still feeling a little shaky on his feet. He had taken the hit, just like Cody said real football players did. But he wasn't feeling good about it.

Out on the field, Hilton Prep gained another first down on a run by T.J. and a short pass to Mike Moretti.

Coach Morris came up to Tim. "Are you ready?"

"I think so." Tim wasn't sure, but there was no way he could just stand on the sidelines.

Coach Morris nodded to Coach Flores. A minute later Coach Flores shouted, "Beeman, go in for Cataldi!"

Tim put on his helmet and ran into the Hilton Prep huddle.

Cody smiled. "Good to see you, Speed. You ready?"

Tim nodded and took a deep breath.

Cody looked around the huddle. "Let's go for it. Maybe we can catch them napping. Fake 34, flanker right post on one."

Tim flared out to the right and eyed the Franklin defensive backs. *Not too close, not too far back. Just about right.*

"Ready...set...hut..."

Tim burst downfield, barely bothering to fake one way or another. He blew by the first defender but saw the Tigers safety coming over to help. Tim looked back. The ball was in the air. The safety reached up. The ball just skimmed his fingertips and dropped into Tim's hands.

The safety fell, and his arms slapped across the back of Tim's legs. Tim stumbled but kept his feet by pressing his left palm against the turf.

There was nothing but green grass in front of him now. He swiftly regained his balance and took off.

Touchdown!

Hilton Prep had cut the lead in half, 14–7. They had a chance.

CHAPTER 15

Tim's touchdown gave his team hope, but it didn't help the Hilton Prep defense stop the Franklin offense.

The Tigers took the following kickoff and moved steadily downfield, grinding out yardage on the ground.

Tim, Cody, and T.J. stood on the sidelines helplessly watching the clock wind down. The three teammates shouted out cheers, hoping against hope that somehow the defense would make a stop.

"Come on, tough defense!"

"Make a play!"

"Hold that line."

The Tigers quarterback spun and handed off to his running back.

This time, Cal dashed from his linebacker spot and met the runner head-on at the line of scrimmage with a thunderous hit. The ball popped loose.

Fumble!

A pile of players scrambled for the bouncing ball. The referee pounced on the pile, trying to determine which team had the football. After a few agonizing seconds, he stood and pointed in the direction of Hilton Prep.

Tim, Cody, T.J., and the entire Hilton Prep sideline leapt into the air. Coach Flores looked at the clock and waved his clipboard high. "Offense, get in there!" he shouted. "Two-minute drill. Got to make some plays!"

Tim glanced at the scoreboard.

Three minutes and twenty-five seconds to play. Seventy yards to go. It wasn't going to be easy.

But Hilton Prep started moving the ball. An eight-yard run by T.J...

A screen pass...

A quick curl in to Tim.

The Vikings got a couple of first downs and moved the ball to midfield.

But then the Franklin defense stiffened. Hilton's run around the left end went nowhere. Then they had an incomplete pass. It was third and ten.

And the clock was still moving—1:22...1:21...1:20...

"We need a big play," Cody said in the huddle and then looked straight at Tim. "Flanker right, down out, and down on one. Got to go get it, Speed."

"Ready...set... hut..."

Tim bolted off the line of scrimmage. He raced ten yards downfield and cut sharply to the right sideline. The Tigers defensive back tried to stay with him. Tim looked back at Cody to sell the fake and then dug his foot into the turf and pivoted up the sideline.

He was open!

Cody threw the ball just before the Franklin defensive line crashed in. The ball was high. And the Franklin safety was coming up fast.

I've got to go get it, Tim thought. *Can't back off this time.*

Tim reached up and grabbed the ball with both hands. He twisted his feet to make sure both were inbounds. But before he could bring his arms down, the Franklin safety crashed into his exposed side at full speed.

Wham!

Tim flew out of bounds, still holding on to the ball. He felt a sharp pain shoot through his side as he thumped to the ground.

Unnnhh!

Tim staggered to his feet and hustled back to the huddle, struggling for his breath. First down at the 20-yard line and things were moving fast.

"Great catch. That's how we go get it!"

Cody said quickly and then called the next play. "Thirty-six pitch on one."

Tim flared out to the right. But the pain in his side was too much. He slumped to one knee before Cody could even start the count. He felt like his chest was on fire.

Coach Flores signaled for a time-out.

Coach Morris and Cal rushed out to help Tim over to the bench. He sat folded over as a cold wind whipped across the sideline.

"Are you okay?"

Tim turned slowly toward the familiar voice. His father was standing behind the bench with the same worried look on his face Tim had seen on Chad Davis's parents' faces at the Hilton Prep varsity game so many weeks ago. Sophia and Marquis were right behind him.

"Y-yeah," Tim gasped, but he knew he wasn't okay. He could barely speak because of the pain in his side. His head dropped and he stared at the dirt.

Tim didn't see the final plays of the game. He didn't see T.J.'s twelve-yard run for a touchdown. Or Cody's pass to Conrad for the two-point conversion.

Tim looked up and saw the final score in the scoreboard lights: 15–14, Hilton Prep.

He heard the shouts of joy all around him. But he kept staring straight down at the hard ground, breathing slowly.

Tim had taken the hit and had helped Hilton win the game, but he didn't feel like celebrating.

CHAPTER 16

Dr. Aylesworth entered the small examining room and smiled. "The good news is you didn't break anything. The X-ray of your ribs was negative."

"Is there some bad news?" Tim's father asked.

Tim already knew the bad news. His ribs and side still hurt like crazy a day after the Franklin game.

"Well, the bad news is that his side is very badly bruised," Dr. Aylesworth said as she sat down in front of a small laptop. "So he's going to be really sore for a few more days."

"When will he be able to play again?" Mr. Beeman asked.

"I would want him to rest the area for at least two or three weeks." She turned to Tim. "How many more games are left in the season?"

"Two. Next Thursday and the week after that."

Dr. Aylesworth shook her head. "Sorry."

Tim's father leaned back in his chair and filled in the silence with the words Tim was already thinking. "Well, that means you're definitely out for the rest of the season."

Tim shrugged. "I guess that's it for football this year." He had just one more question for the doctor. "When can I start running again?"

"In a couple of weeks or so," she said. "If you don't feel any pain when you do it. But take it easy. Start slowly and then build up." Then her tone got serious. "But absolutely no contact sports like basketball or soccer for at least three weeks. And *definitely* no football."

As Tim and his father drove home, Tim's phone pinged with text messages from Cal and T.J.

How r u?

Out 4 season

2 bad
Heard u r hurt.

Bruised ribs.
Out 4 season.

Ouch! C u @ school.

Cody was sitting on the Beemans' front step when they pulled into the driveway.

Tim eased out of the car carefully. "What are you doing here?" he called to Cody.

"T.J. and Cal texted me that you were out for the season." Cody stood up. "I was just checking on my favorite receiver."

Mr. Beeman unlocked the front door and invited Cody in.

"It stinks that you got hurt," Cody said as he followed Tim and Mr. Beeman into the living room. "You had one of your best games against Franklin." He took out his phone and clicked on the team stats. "And you were the leading receiver for the season," he said, turning the phone so Tim could see. "By a mile."

Passing:

	Games	C/Atts	Yards	TDs	INTs
Lewis	6	48/98	761	6	3
Hansen	1	0/1	0	0	0

Rushing:

	Games	Atts.	Yards	TDs
Jackson	6	115	603	8
Allen	6	28	112	1
Lewis	6	19	62	1

Receiving:

	Games	Recs.	Yards	TDs
Beeman	6	24	448	4
Moretti	6	11	138	0
Nowak	6	8	103	1
Jackson	6	5	72	1

"There are two more games left," Tim said. "Someone could still catch me."

"No way!" Cody laughed. "I'd have to throw Moretti a hundred passes for him to catch you."

"You guys want anything to drink?" Tim's father called from the kitchen.

"No thanks, Mr. Beeman. I'm cool."

"I'll take a ginger ale," Tim told his dad. He sat down slowly and leaned his head against the back of the sofa.

Cody went right back to his favorite subject—football. "At least the Franklin game wasn't a total loss," he said, eyeing Tim. "I saw the Hawk at the game."

"Really?"

"Yeah, I bet he's thinking about bringing you up to varsity next season to play wide receiver...to take Chad Davis's place."

"Is Chad playing again?" Tim asked.

Cody nodded. "Oh, yeah. He just missed a game or two. But it doesn't matter. Chad will be gone next year, and with your speed you're going to make everybody forget about Chad Davis."

"I doubt that," Tim said softly. "Anyway, I'm not so sure I want to play varsity next year."

Mr. Beeman came in with Tim's ginger ale. "You'll be moving up to varsity next year, won't you, Cody?" he asked.

"Yeah, I'll be a junior. Same as T.J. and Cal and a bunch of other guys." Cody turned and looked at Tim. "So you may not want to stay on JV. I mean, there's nothing better than varsity football at Hilton Prep. Think about it. You, me, T.J., and Cal. Friday night...under the lights."

Tim *had* been thinking about it. He'd been thinking about it ever since he'd seen Chad Davis lying on the ground. Ever since he'd backed off that last pass in the King game. Ever since he'd been hit really hard on the field. He'd thought about it during every game and every cold, dark practice.

Sometimes it was all he thought about.

"It's not just whether I play varsity or JV..." Tim took a deep breath and forced himself to finish. "I'm...I'm just not sure I want to play football at all next year."

"Not play football?" Cody blurted out. "What are you talking about?"

Mr. Beeman studied his son carefully from across the room. "Maybe you should wait until the end of the season to make that decision."

"It's already the end of *my* season," Tim said. "Remember?"

Cody started in, seeming almost desperate to keep his favorite receiver. "You're injured. Nobody likes to be—"

"It's not that."

"Then what is it?" his father asked gently.

Tim thought about it all for a moment. He could sense their questioning looks. He knew what he felt, but it was hard to put his feelings into words.

"I guess I've realized that I'm not really a football player," he began. "I'm just a guy who can run fast."

"You mean like Bob Hayes and Darrell Green?" his father asked.

"That's the point, Dad," Tim said. "They were *real* football players. They *liked* to play." Tim paused and then added, "I don't really like to play."

"But you're the best receiver on the team!" Cody almost shouted.

Tim could see the disappointment on his father's face, so he looked away. His eye settled on a picture of his mother on an end table across the room.

Tim realized he had to make this decision

for himself. Not for his mom. Or his dad. Or for Cody, T.J., Cal, or any of the other guys on the team.

Just for himself.

"I tried," Tim said, almost swallowing his words. "I gave it my best shot. I know I can play and I like being with the team and all, but...I don't really like the game."

Cody leaned back in his chair, shaking his head as if he simply could not understand what he was hearing. He stared at the statistics on his phone one more time, his shoulders slumped. "Don't like football?" he whispered in disbelief.

When Tim didn't respond, Cody looked up hopefully and tried again. "Come on, man. Maybe you just haven't...you know... given it enough time. I mean you're the best receiver we got. Tell me you'll think about it some more."

"I don't need to think about it any longer. I know what I want to do."

After a few moments of awkward silence, Tim's father spoke up. "All right, all right. I think I know where you're coming from," he said. "You're a good player, but you don't enjoy the game." He sat back in his chair. "You're old enough to make your own decisions. And I have to admit, you did give it a good shot."

Then he looked at Tim and pointed a finger as if he was warning him. "But I want you to do some kind of sport," he said firmly. "I don't want you hanging around the house after school doing nothing."

"Yeah," Cody said. "What are you going to do without football?"

"Don't worry," Tim said. "I'll do something. I promise."

Tim glanced over at the picture of his mother again.

Somehow she seemed to be smiling right at him.

CHAPTER 17

A few weeks later, Tim stood on the Hilton Prep indoor track, bouncing up and down on the balls of his feet, waiting.

Marquis was running toward him with a baton in his hand.

"Come on, Marquis! Pick it up!"

Tim thought about what Coach Levitt had taught him about the exchange of the baton.

Get a head start...reach back with your left hand...switch the baton to your right as soon as you can.

As Marquis got closer, Tim started off slowly. The other teams were making their exchanges in the other lanes. Tim knew he would have his work cut out for him to pass them.

"You can do it, Speed!" Sophia shouted from the infield.

Tim reached back as Marquis slapped the baton into his left hand. Within a single step, Tim switched it to his right hand.

Tim watched the three runners ahead of him. *I only have a hundred yards to catch them,* he thought. *I'd better turn it on.* He took off, reaching deep inside himself for every ounce of speed.

In fifty yards he had cut the lead in half. Tim could hear the crowd in the Hilton arena cheering, urging him on. He flashed by two runners and set his sights on the leader, still a few stubborn yards ahead.

Twenty-five yards to go...twenty yards... fifteen...

The distance to the finish line was disappearing as quickly as if Tim were on a long touchdown run toward the end zone.

Tim pulled alongside the last runner with ten yards to go. He squeezed out a final burst of strength and speed, leaned out his chest toward the tape, and flashed across the finish line almost stride for stride with the other runner. He felt the tape touch his chest.

The crowd burst into cheers. The other three Hilton Prep relay runners jumped up and down near the finish line, slapping each other's shoulders. Then they shook hands with the other teams.

Coach Levitt pushed past the other runners. "You did it, you did it!" he shouted to Tim. "You won by a tenth of a second!"

Tim leaned over at his waist to try to catch his breath. Even though it had just been a few weeks since the Franklin Prep game, the pain in his side was completely gone. He straightened up and nodded to his coach, relieved to hear that it was official— he had crossed the line first.

Tim easily picked out his father in the small crowd, where he was giving Tim the thumbs-up sign. Tim waved to him and headed over to join a group of his teammates in the infield.

"Whoa, that was too close," Sophia said.

"I didn't think you were going to catch that last guy."

"No worries," Marquis said with a wave of his hand. "We had him all the way."

"What do you mean *we?*" Tim said, raising an eyebrow. "I seem to recall that I was in fourth place when you handed me the baton."

"But it was a great exchange," Marquis protested, holding his arms wide. "You've got to give me that."

Tim laughed and then looked at Sophia. "Any idea how we're doing?"

"Coach said we're in second place because of your 4x100 win." She smiled. "You're helping the team big-time, Speed."

Tim smiled. "When do you race?"

"I've got the 800 in about ten minutes. What about you?"

"The 200 finals in half an hour."

"You'll blow them away." Sophia checked her phone for the time. "You might have a little time to work on your math homework. I'll help you after my race."

Tim pulled his math textbook out of his

backpack. He looked up and saw his father sitting cross-legged in the mostly empty stands, reading the newspaper.

Coach Levitt dropped by the infield, still charged up about the relay win. "Good job, Tim," he said. "But you can get even better with more practice. We'll work on your stride. It's a little ragged in spots. Don't worry, though. You've got the makings of a first-class sprinter." As he walked away, he called back, "Now, relax and get ready for the 200!"

Tim stretched out on the infield in his track warm-up suit and opened his math book. It was dry and warm inside the Hilton indoor track bubble. There was no one chasing him or hitting him or trying to throw him to the ground. No plays to memorize and no pressure to pick up extra yardage.

Just another race to run. As fast as he could. Like a speed demon.

Tim smiled to himself. For the first time since he'd come to Hilton Prep, he felt like he was in the right spot. He felt happy and at home.

CHAPTER 18

Tim was a little late getting to the Hilton Prep lunchroom. He looked around for Sophia and Marquis.

"Hey, Tim, over here!" Cody was waving him over to the center of the room as he had done so many months before.

At the same moment Tim spotted Sophia and Marquis sitting at the track team table. Tim turned and made his way over to the football table.

"Hey, Speed! Where've you been?" Cody shouted over the cafeteria noise. "Seems like you've been avoiding us ever since you got hurt."

Tim slipped into a chair. "I just figured since I wasn't going to be on the football team I'd sit with some of the track kids."

Cody waved off the thought. "What are you talking about?" he said. "Once a football player, always a football player. You're always welcome around here. You're still one of us."

"Yeah." T.J. nodded. "It's like being a marine—"

"Or a priest," Ashley said with a laugh.

Cody ignored her remark and tapped Tim with the back of his hand. "Tell you what, Speed. Why don't you bring some of your track buddies over here?" He looked around the table. "I'm getting tired of hanging with just this crowd."

Alexis glared at him. "What do you mean *you're* getting tired of *us?*"

"You sure?" Tim asked.

"Yeah, we could use a change of pace. Shake up the lineup."

Tim agreed and headed toward the track table.

"Hey, Tim!" Marquis called. "Grab a seat."

"Where's your lunch?" Sophia asked.

"Over at the football table."

"Oh," Sophia said. "You going big-time today?"

"Not exactly." Tim looked over his shoulder. "Cody wants us to come over and sit at their table today."

"Really?" Sophia straightened up in her chair.

"Yeah." Tim lowered his voice as if he were telling his friends a secret. "Just don't pay attention to everything Cody says. He's really a good guy."

Sophia and Marquis stood and picked up their lunch trays. "Don't worry," Sophia said. "We can handle Cody."

"All right, make room, boys and girls," Cody said as the three approached the table. "We've got some track stars in the house."

Tim, Sophia, and Marquis sat down as Cody handled the introductions. "Ashley and Alexis, you know Sophia and Marquis. They're the folks who stole my favorite wide receiver from the football team."

"We didn't steal him," Sophia protested. "He decided that one all on his own."

"Well, I'm not so sure about that. But I'm

warning you right here, right now," Cody said, wagging his finger at Sophia. "We're gonna steal him back. You watch."

"Don't be so sure," Tim said.

"You know you can do both...football *and* track," Calvin said.

"That's true," Sophia agreed. She eyed Calvin's thick arms. "So why don't you help us out with the shot put? You look like you'd be strong enough."

Calvin tilted his head, clearly enjoying Sophia's compliment. "Maybe I will," he said. "Maybe I will."

"What about you, T.J.?" Marquis asked, looking across the table. "We can always use another fast runner."

"Wait a minute," T.J. said, leaning back and holding up his hands. "I'm not as fast as Speed here."

"That's okay. They give points for second and third place. We can use all the points we can get."

"What about us?" Ashley asked, pointing to Alexis and herself. "We've been doing some running."

"Wait...wait!" Cody held up his hands before Sophia could answer. "You're stealing my whole table."

Tim laughed. "They're not stealing anybody," he said. "They're just letting them make up their own minds."

Cody looked straight at Tim. "Oh, you mean like the way you made up your own mind that you didn't want to play football?"

"Yeah." Tim looked around the crowded table of smiling friends and teammates. "Just like that."

THE REAL STORY

"BULLET" BOB HAYES

Very few men can claim to be the fastest man in the National Football League (NFL). Even fewer can claim to be the world's fastest human.

In the 1960s, Bob Hayes could claim to be both.

In October 1964, the twenty-one-year-old Hayes stood in lane one of the Olympic Stadium track in Tokyo, Japan, waiting for the start of the 100-meter final. It was the worst lane assignment because an earlier walking race had chewed up the cinders on that part of the track, making it soft and difficult to run on.

It hardly mattered. Hayes burst out of the starting blocks and pulled away from the field, winning the gold medal easily with a world record time of ten seconds flat.

Days later, Hayes stood on the same track, waiting to run the final leg of the 4x100-meter relay race. He was several steps behind when he received the baton from the third American sprinter. Hayes turned on the burners, flashing by the other runners to win another gold medal. He had run the final one hundred yards in an unbelievable 8.6 seconds!

There was no doubt about it. Hayes was the world's fastest human.

The appearances Hayes made at the Tokyo Olympics were his last as a track athlete. But Hayes was also a terrific football player.

He starred as a running back at Florida A&M, a historically black college. The Dallas Cowboys drafted Hayes in the seventh round of the 1964 NFL draft and switched him to wide receiver.

With his blinding speed, Hayes changed pro football. In his first two seasons, he led the NFL in receiving touchdowns while averaging more than twenty yards per catch.

Coaches changed their defenses against Hayes because no one could cover "Bullet Bob" man-to-man. New York Giants defensive back Dick Lynch recalled years later, "Fans used to boo me when he got behind me, but how can you cover him running backward when he's the fastest guy in the world?"

So teams began to play zone defenses in which the defensive backs and linebackers covered certain areas of the field rather than any particular player. But not even these new defenses could stop Hayes. In his sixth and seventh seasons with the Cowboys, he led the NFL in yards per reception, ripping off an amazing 26.1 and 24 yards per catch.

Eventually injuries slowed Hayes down, and he retired after eleven NFL seasons and seventy-six career touchdowns. Hayes struggled with alcohol and drug problems outside the spotlight of pro football. He was inducted into the NFL Hall of Fame in 2009, seven years after his death. Hayes is still the only man to have won both an Olympic gold medal and a Super Bowl ring.

OTHER SPEED DEMONS

There have been other speed demons on the gridiron over the years. Running backs—from Red Grange in the 1920s to Chris Johnson in the twenty-first century—have used their breakaway speed to dazzle fans.

It's the same with wide receivers. Teams love to have speedsters who can stretch the field and force the defense to defend against the long bomb. So through the years teams have drafted track stars such as Joey Galloway, Willie Gault, and Cliff Branch to get behind defenders and race to the end zone. While at the University of Colorado, Branch won the NCAA championship for the 100-meter dash. Gault qualified for the 1980 Olympics.

With so many high-octane receivers, NFL teams also needed defensive backs with speed. Two of the fastest were Deion Sanders and Darrell Green. Green won the NFL's Fastest Man competition a record four times when the contest was held in the 1980s and 1990s. In fact, Green never lost the competition in which the fastest NFL players competed against each other in the 60-yard dash.

But these speed demons weren't just sprinters. Green played cornerback for the Washington Redskins for twenty seasons. He made seven Pro Bowls and, like Sanders, was selected for the Pro Football Hall of Fame. Galloway, Gault, and Branch all enjoyed long careers terrorizing NFL defenses.

As Tim discovered, it takes more than just speed to excel at football. It's a rough game. No matter how fast you are, somebody is going to catch you. You have to be able to take the hits. But perhaps most important, you have to want to play in order to be a real football player.

ACKNOWLEDGMENTS

The information concerning Bob Hayes and some of the other speed demons of the National Football League came from *Top 10 Fastest Players of All Time,* a film by NFL Films. I also got some details about Hayes from his September 20, 2002, obituary published in the *New York Times* and written by Frank Litsky.

I watched the film of Hayes's incredible 100-meter and 4x100-meter gold medal runs on YouTube.

The statistics about the various players are from the wonderful website at *Pro-Football-Reference.com.*

My son, Liam Bowen, who is the Associate Head Baseball Coach at the University of Maryland–Baltimore County (UMBC), advised me about plausible times for a fast fourteen-year-old to run various distances.

As always, Steve Willertz, a friend and former youth football coach, drew the play diagrams.

ABOUT THE AUTHOR

Fred Bowen was a Little Leaguer who loved to read. Now he is the author of many action-packed books of sports fiction. He has also written a weekly sports column for kids in the *Washington Post* since 2000.

Fred played lots of sports growing up, including soccer at Marblehead High School. For thirteen years, he coached kids' baseball, soccer, and basketball teams. Some of his stories spring directly from his coaching experience and his sports-happy childhood in Marblehead, Massachusetts.

Fred holds a degree in history from the University of Pennsylvania and a law degree from George Washington University. He was a lawyer for many years before retiring to become a full-time children's author. Bowen has been a guest author at schools and conferences across the country, as well as the

Smithsonian Institute in Washington, D.C., and The Baseball Hall of Fame.

Fred lives in Silver Spring, Maryland, with his wife, Peggy Jackson. Their son is a college baseball coach, and their daughter is a reading teacher in Washington, D.C.

For more information check out the author's website at *www.fredbowen.com*.

MORE FROM FRED BOWEN

PB: $6.95 • HC: $14.95

 **BASEBALL**

Dugout Rivals
PB: 978-1-56145-515-7

ke Daley loves baseball. He
ves playing for the Red Sox in
e Woodside baseball league.
loves playing short stop.
ost of all, he loves to win.

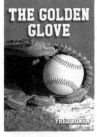

The Golden Glove
PB: 978-1-56145-505-8

Without his lucky glove, Jamie
doesn't believe in his ability to
lead his baseball team to victory.

The Kid Coach
PB: 978-1-56145-506-5

Scott and his teammates can't
find an adult to coach their
team, so they must find a leader
among themselves.

Lucky Enough
PB: 978-1-56145-958-2
HC: 978-1-56145-957-5

ey is overjoyed when his lucky
arm helps him make the travel
am, but will his luck hold out?

Perfect Game
PB: 978-1-56145-625-3
HC: 978-1-56145-701-4

Isaac learns the true meaning
of a perfect game when he
volunteers with a team of
developmentally disabled
players.

Playoff Dreams
PB: $6.95 / 978-1-56145-507-2

Brendan is one of the best
players in the league, but no
matter how hard he tries, he
can't make his team win.

T. J.'s Secret Pitch
PB: 978-1-56145-504-1

T.J. is smaller than his teammates and his pitches just don't have the power to get batters out. When he learns about 1940s player Rip Sewell, he may have found a solution.

Throwing Heat
PB: 978-1-56145-540-9
HC: 978-1-56145-573-7

Jack has a sizzling fastball, but does he have what it takes to pitch his team to victory?

Winners Take All
PB: 978-1-56145-512-6

In order to win an important baseball game, twelve-year-old Kyle claims to have made a difficult catch, which he actually dropped.

 SOCCER

Go for the Goal
PB: 978-1-56145-632-1

Josh and his talented travel league soccer teammates are having trouble coming together as a successful team.

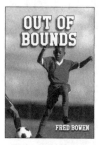

Out of Bounds
PB: 978-1-56145-894-3
HC: 978-1-56145-845-5

Can Nate discover the importance of good sportsmanship?

Soccer Team Upset
PB: 978-1-56145-495-2

Tyler's hopes for an unbeatable season for the Cougars disappear when his friend Zack, the team's hot-shot midfielder, and two more of their best players accept an offer to play for an elite travel team.

🏀 BASKETBALL

The Final Cut
PB: 978-1-56145-510-2

ur friends who share a love of sketball have to go through youts for the school team. But ll they all make the team?

Full Court Fever
PB: 978-1-56145-508-9

The Falcons have the skill but not the height required to win their games. Will they be able to win the dreaded end-of-the-season game against their much taller rivals?

Hardcourt Comeback
PB: 978-1-56145-516-4

When a basketball team's star forward loses his confidence, he has to learn how to think like a winner again.

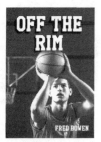

Off the Rim
PB: 978-1-56145-509-6

ll Chris ever be more than a nchwarmer?

On the Line
PB: 978-1-56145-511-9

Marcus is the high scorer and best rebounder on his basketball team, but he's not so great at free throws.

Outside Shot
PB: 978-1-56145-956-8
HC: 978-1-56145-955-1

Eighth-grader Richie Mallon has always known he was a shooter, but will his amazing shooting talent be enough to keep him on the team?

FOOTBALL

Real Hoops
PB: 978-1-56145-566-9

Can street ball and technical play mix it up on the court and score wins for the team?

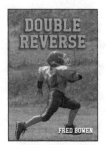

Double Reverse
PB: 978-1-56145-807-3
HC: 978-1-56145-814-1

Jesse is experienced as a wide receiver—but can he play against type and help his new team as a quarterback?

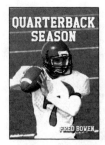

Quarterback Season
PB: 978-1-56145-594-2

Matt Monroe is a shoo-in for starting quarterback for the Parkside Middle School football team this year. Or is he?

Touchdown Trouble
PB: 978-1-56145-497-6

Sam loves football. Most of all he loves the feeling he gets when his team, the Cowboys, are working together—moving closer and closer to the end zone.

Speed Demon
HC: 978-1-68263-076-1
PB: 978-1-68263-077-8

Eager to find his place at his elite new school, Tim Beeman is torn between running track and trying out for football.